ELBURG,

THE KINGDOM OF UNDERSEA

-Where, the power is abducted.

On a Drowsy Sunday morning a woman in a long dark skirt hesitated in front of a house on a tree lined Street. She hadn't parked a car nor had she come by taxi. No neighbor had seen her strolling along the sidewalk. She simply appeared, as if stepping between one shadow and the next. The women Walked to the door and lifted her fist to knock.

Inside the house, *Sia* sat on the living room rug and ate chicken sticks from the microwave and dragged through sludge of ketchup.
Her twin sister, *Maria*, napped on the couch curled around a blanket thumb in her fruit punch stained mouth. And on the door end of the sofa their elder sister *Genevieva* stared at the

television screen, her gaze was fixed on the cartoon mouse as it ran from the cartoon cat. She laughed when it seems as if the mouse was about to get eaten.

Genny was different from other big sisters, but since seven years old Sia and Maria were identical with the same Shaggy blonde hair and diamond shaped faces they were different too. Maria yawned and stretched, pressing her cheek against Genny's knee. Outside, the sun was shining, scorching the asphalt of driveways. Lawn mower engines whirled and the children splashed in backyard pools. Dad was in the outbuilding where he had a forge. Mom was in the kitchen cooking hamburgers. Everything was boring, everything was fine.

When the knock came, Sia hoped up to answer it. She hoped it might be one of the girls from across the street wanting to play video games or inviting her for an after dinner swim.

The tall women stood on the mat, glaring down at her. She wore a brown leather jacket despite The Heat. Her shoes were shot with silver and they rang hollowly as she stepped over the threshold. Sia looked up into her Shadow face and shivered. "Mom", she yelled."Moooooooooom, someone's here". Her mother came from the kitchen, wiping wet hands on her jeans. When

she saw the women she went pale."Go to your room", she told Sia in a scary voice. "Now!."
"Whose child is that?" The women asked, pointing at her. Her voice was hardly accented."Yours? His? ".
" No one's ," Mom didn't even look in Sia's direction." She's no one's child. "
That wasn't right. Sia and Maria looked just like their dad. Everyone said so.
She took a few steps towards the stairs but didn't want to be alone in her room. Genny, Sia thought.
Genny will know who the tall woman is. Genny will know what to do.
But Sia couldn't seen to make herself move any farther.
"I have seen many impossible things", the woman said."I have seen the acorn before the oak. I have seen the spark before the flame. But never have I seen such as this: a dead women living. A child born from nothing"
Mom seemed at a loss for words. Her body was vibrating with tension. Sia wanted to take her hand and squeeze it, but she didn't dare.

"I doubted 'Roa' when she told me I'd find you here" said the woman, her voice softening.
"The bones of an Earthly woman and her unborn

child in the burn remains of our estate weren't convincing. Do you know what it is to return from battle to find your wife dead your only heir with her? And my blood brother faced it only because of you"

Mom shook her head, not as if she was answering her, but as though she was trying to shake off the words.

She took a step towards mom, and mom took a step back. There was something wrong with the tall women's leg. She moved stiffly, as though it hurt her. The light was different in the entry hall and Sia could see the odd green tint of the woman's skin and the way her lower teeth seen too large for her mouth.

She was able to see that the women's eyes were like Genny's.

"I was never going to be happy with *Haleth*" mom told her. "Your world isn't for people like me"

The tall women regarded her for a long moment, "you made vows" she said finally.

Her gaze went to Sia and her expression hardened. "What is a promise for a mortal wife worth?"

Mom turned. At her mother's look Sia dashed into the living room.

Maria was still sleeping. That television was still on. Genevieva looked up with half lidded cat eyes. "Who's at the door?" She asked "I heard arguing."

"A Scary woman", Sia told her out of breath even though she'd barely run at all. Her heart was pounding. "We are supposed to go upstairs" She didn't care that mom told only her to go upstairs. She wasn't going by herself. With a sigh, Genny unfolded from the couch and shook Maria awake. Drowsily Sia's twin followed them into the hallway.

As they started toward the carpet covered steps, Sia Saw her father come in from the back garden. He held an axe in his hand Forged to be a near replica of one he studied in a museum in Iceland. It wasn't weird to see dad with an axe. He and his friends were into old weapons and would spend a lot of time talking about material culture and sketching ideas for fantastical blades. What was odd was the way he held the weapon as if he was going to....

Her father swung the axe towards the tall women.

He had never raised the hand to discipline Sia or her sisters, even when they got into big trouble. He wouldn't hurt anyone, he just wouldn't.

And yet. And yet.

The axe went past the tall women, bidding into the wood trim of the door.

Maria made and odd, high keening noise and slapped her palms over her mouth.
The tall women drew a curved blade from beneath her leather coat. A sword, like from a story book. Dad was trying to pull the axe free from the door frame when the women plunged the sword into that stomach pushing it upward. There was a sound like stick snapping, and animal cry.
Dad felt to the vestibule carpet, the one mom always yelled about when they tracked mud on it. The rug, that was turning red.
Mom screamed. Sia screamed, Maria and Genny screamed. Everyone seemed to be screaming except the tall women.
"Come here" she said, looking directly at Genny.
"Y-you monster "their mother shouted, moving towards the kitchen. "He's dead!, do not run from me, "the women tall her, "not after what you have done if you run again I swear I...."
But she did run. She was almost around the corner when her blade stuck her in the back. She crumpled into the linoleum falling arms knocking magnets off the fridge.

The smell of fresh blood was heavy in the air like wet, hot metal.

Sia ran at the woman, slamming her fist against her chest, kicking at her legs. She wasn't even scared. She wasn't sure she felt anything at all. The women paid Sia no mind. For a long moment, she just stood there as though she couldn't quite believe what she has done. As though she was she could take back the last 5 minutes. Then she sank to one knee and got hold of Sia's shoulders. The woman pinned her arms on Sia's sides as she couldn't hit her anymore, but she wasn't even looking at her.

Her gaze was on Genevieva.

"You were stolen from me" she told her.

"I have come to take you to your true home, in **Elburg**, *the kingdom of undersea* beneath the *north dale* ocean. There, you will be rich beyond measures. There, you will be with your own kind."

"No" Genny told her in her little voice "I am never going anywhere with you"

"I am your aunt", the women told her, voice harsh, raising like the crack of a Lash. "you are our only heir and my brother's blood. Your father, Haleth needs you desperately and you will obey me in this as in all things"

She didn't move but her jaw set.

"You are not her blood" Sia shouted at the

women. Even though she and Genny had the same eyes, she wouldn't let herself believe it.

Woman's grip Tightened on her shoulders, and she made a little squeezed squeeking sound, but she stared up defiantly. She'd won plenty of staring contest.

The women looked away first, turning to watch Maria, on her knees, shaking mom while she sobbed, as though she was trying to wake her up. Mom didn't move. Mom and dad were dead. They were never going to move again.

"I hate you," Genny proclaimed to the tall women with a viciousness that Sia was glad of."I will always hate you, I vow it"

The women's stony expression didn't change. "Nonetheless, you will come with me. Ready these little humans. Pack light. we will ride before dark.

Genevieva's chin came up, "leave them alone if you have to take me but not them"

She is there at Genny and snorted, "you'd protect your sisters from me, would you?, Tell me then where would you have them go?"

Genny don't answer. They had no grandparents, no leaving family at all, at least none they know. She look at Sia again, released her shoulders and rose to her feet.

"They are the progeny of my brother's wife and

thus my responsibility. I may be cruel a monster and a murderer that do not shrink my responsibilities. Not should you shrink you're as the eldest."

Years later, when Sia told the story of what happened, she couldn't recall the part where they packed. Shock seemed to have erased that hour entirely. Somehow Genny must have found bags, must have put in their favorite picture books and their beloved toys along with the photographs and pajamas and coats and shirts. Or maybe Sia head packed for herself. She can't imagine how it had felt, and as the years went by, she could make herself feel it again. The horror of the murders dulled with time. Her memories of the day blurred.

A black horse was nibbling the grass of the lawn when they went outside. Sia wanted to throw her arms around its neck and press her wet face into its silky mane. Before she could, the tall women swung her and Maria across the saddle handling them like baggage rather than children. She put Genny up behind her. "hold on "she said.
She rode all the back town way she rode through

the Woods, through the bushes and through the hills. The horse stopped near a valley and got them down. From there she took the children on their feet the way between the valleys ended at a ocean.

Maria nodded, "northdale" as she remember the place from the map of her book cover. The woman credited, "yes, north dale Ocean now we have to go beneath this"

"But how can we go underneath the sea, we would die out of breath "asked Sia with frightened eyes.

"Obviously you can't survive under sea but Genny can, because she is our kind" the woman look at Genny.

"But I can't let my sisters here, like this, to die..."Genny, was going to speak but the woman's movements stopped her to complete her sentence.

The woman took a bottle out of her pocket. It was sparkling, however the bottle was transparent but the thing in it was glittery.

The woman gave that to the twin sisters and told them to eat it. They both were confused as well surprised. Then the woman told them "this is the pollen of coral this will allow you to survive under the water"

The women asked Genny to jump in the water

but Genny was scared of water from her childhood. Her mother never allowed her even for swimming. Genny hesitantly denied to her. Then forcibly the women pushed Genny into water.

Frightened Genny was breathless in water and she was fighting for air. The woman told her to speak " *ik Ben zeemeermim*"

Desperately optionless Genny repeated those magical words.

On the exact movement Genny's mortal body commences to change, her pale, smooth legs turned to a glittery vibrant aqua green coloured tail just as they have seen Aerial in TV had. Sia and Maria were surprised to see their elder sister to be turning as a mermaid. The women insisted the twins to jump. Confused Sia question her, "who are you and what are you trying to do with us?"

"I would have told you earlier but myself *Dolreth*, aunt of your elder sister (sister of Genny's father)"the women introduced herself. Maria asked her,"but where are you taking us to?"

"You'll know it, now come with me, jump!" she said and jumped in the ocean along with them. She too got a tail of cobalt blue similar to Genny, although they were of same kind. But the point was Sia and Maria were human blood so their physical state remained unchanged, but they were able to breathe under water with the help of that glittery coral pollen.

The woman, (Dolreth) asserted them to follow her underwater. They dived deep into the sea. It was just like a dream or a fantasy to those three little girls to whizz in the water. Those deep sea creatures were fascinating. Groups of fishes, little turtles, ink octopus, giant isopods, shrimps, blue tangs, colourful, vibrant, shiny, and different naturally designed kinds of flora and fauna have stolen their past hours. The view was a feast for eyes; Maria was completely submerged with the surroundings. Sia as for her nature, she was looking for sharks,but Genny was still astonished to a have a tail like full of mermaid. There the women found a seahorse and told them to sit on it. Genny and Maria together sat on one and Sia sat with Dolreth. They travelled under the deepest grooves of the ocean.

She took them into the Abyss of the ocean, where light had no way to enter, darkness was only a hope and black was not a color to indicate that. Three girls gone blind, nothing seemed until the light came up within the spinal of jelly fishes. The speed of seahorses increased, it was like they were travelling into another dimension, but it passed just in moments and they entered into a complete different place.

Sia's mouth was put opened, Maria's eyes were startled, and Genny was amazed.

"Land under water???" They three shocked at once.

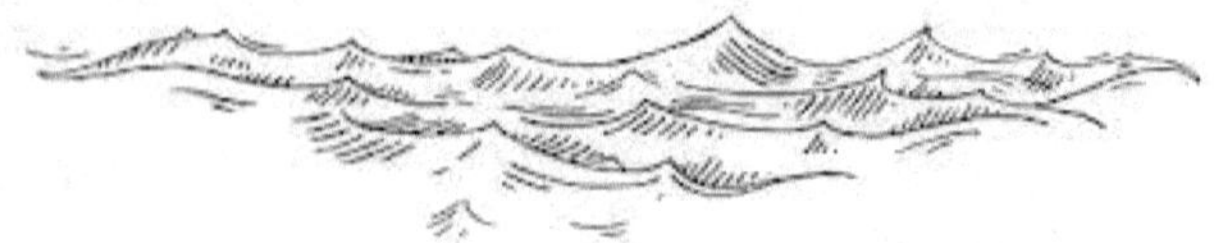

"Welcome to Elburg, the kingdom of undersea."

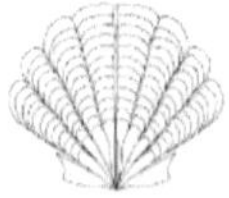

I sit on a couch; it was actually a purple coral. I got my hair braided and adorned with a star shaped ornament which was actually so pretty that I have never seen in our world. My face was glowing up when I looked into mirror and from behind I can see a creature, Miss Roa my room maker, has brought me some grass tea. She put it on a wooden table which was not a wood of tree bark but was a kind of root wood found in the middle depth of Ocean. After having my tea I went down stairs that I could see my elder sister Genevieva but instead of finding Genny I saw Maria adorned in a French blue colour dress and staring Haleth having a discussion with one of his knight.
It has been 10 years of us being in the kingdom of undersea but still Maria's nature hasn't changed.

I still remember when Dolreth brought us to Elburg and left us in the court of *Haleth*, the

biological father of Genny.
Genny being his first heir, he took much care of her not just her but he took care of me and Maria too as we are his step daughters he never uncared his responsibility for us. Even though, Haleth looked so scary and hard but he never forced Genny for anything. Genny has been given everything, wealth, power, control and yet she hated Haleth and Elburg.

Although ,Genny belongs to the folk of Elburg itself. She too got magic like the people of undersea had. People here may appear normal with human physical body but they possess a different kind of physical state of being a mermaid or mermen with a tail whenever they enter brink of water. I was so wondered at the beginning to find a normal land underwater, where Ocean is the sky and fishes are stars.

"Sia" shouted Maria, I was actually drowned in my own thoughts of how I felt when I was taken to undersea kingdom.
Maria shouted again and asked me to go to her as she was so lazy. "What was the talk going?"I asked her as I knew she was hearing all the talk. "Relations of Haleth with high court aren't good enough" she told me as a conclusion of their

discussion.
"Oh! But where is Genny?"I diverted her talk.
"She might be in her room, if you want then go, I'm going to my room and I am so hungry "she said in a desperate voice.

The way to Genny's room from hall was not so far, but my thoughts were like what would be the problem of Haleth with high court.

Although high king is the emperor of Elburg and every creature of undersea kingdom should obey him. Haleth and some others are the kings of their own estates divided in Elburg. They all are under high king's dominion.
I was searching for Genny in her room but I didn't found her there. I was searching for her all over the house. The interior of Haleth's house is whitewashed plaster and massive rough-cut wooden beams. The glass panes in the windows are stained gray as trapped smoke, making the light strange. As I go down the spiral Stairs I spot Genny hiding in a little balcony, frowning over a comic's zine stolen from the human world.
Genny grins at me. She is in jeans and a billowy shirt. Being Haleth's legitimate daughter, she feels no pressure to please him. She does what

she likes. Including reading magazines that might have iron staples rather than blue binding their pages, not carrying if her fingers get singed.

"Heading somewhere?" she asks me softly.

"Just was searching for you" I sighed after all finding her in such a big house.

When we first came here, Maria and Genny and I would huddle in is Genny's big bed and talk about what we remember from home. We'd talk about the meals mom burned and the popcorn dad made. Our next door neighbor's names, the way the house smelled, what school was like, the holidays, the taste of icing on birthday cakes. The talk about the shows with watched hatching the plots recalling the dialogue until all over memories were polished to smooth and false.

"Where is Maria?" She asked me. "As usual in her room, having food" I exclaimed.

"Aren't you going school today?" Genny quires even after knowing that i hate going there. The moment I realize I have to go, i turned back to call Maria for school. After all Genny does learn some magic and she neither wanted to go to undersea school nor did she.

"You should come" I tell her. "Maria is in a weird mood"

Genny gives me a speculative look and then shake her head as a denial."I've got other plans "she told, which might mean she is going to sneak over the mortal world for the evening or it might means she is going to spend in on the balcony, reading.

Either way, if it annoys Haleth, it pleases Genny.

When I was back the way I saw he is waiting for us in the hall with his second wife, *Tulie*. Her skin is in Bluish colour of skim milk and her hair is as white as fresh fallen snow. She is beautiful but unnerving to look at,like a ghost. Haleth is dressed in green, the colour of deep forest. His sword at his hip is no ornament.
"You both look well," Haleth says,i turns to see whom he included as both, there I saw Maria standing behind me, the warmth of his tone making the words as rare compliment. His gaze goes to the stairs." Is your sister on her way?" He hopes Genny to comedown for breakfast.
"I don't know" i lie. Lying is so easy here. I can do it all day long and never be caught. "she must have forgotten "I says.
Disappointment passes over Haleth's face, but not surprise. He had outside to say something to the hob holding the reins.

We sat on dinner table for dine. Everyone having their eyes on plates but Tulie's words took attention "Be careful tonight", Tulie says. "Promise me you will neither eat nor drink nor dance." She reminds us of a ceremony in High court we're going tonight.
"We've been to court before," i remind her.
" But you children are forgetful "she sneers. Haleth married her seven years ago, and shortly after, she gave him a child,a sickly boy named *Hue*, with tiny adorable horns on his head. It has always been clear the Tulie puts up with me and Maria only for haleth's sake. She seems to think of us as her husband's favoured hounds.
Hue thinks of us as sisters, which I can tell, makes Tulie nervous even though I would never do anything to hurt him.
"You are under Haleth's protection, remember this", with that little speech complete, She walks out.

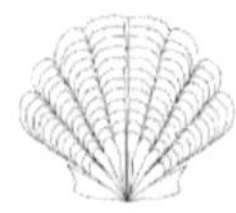

As the day passed, night began to rise. Here night doesn't remind me of dark sky but of dark water, with shiny fishes indicating stars.

We have been called down stairs, as usually Genny wasn't interested. Tulie asserted us to follow her for the ceremony and then back home.
Maria and I share a look and then follow her. Haleth is already seated on a largest of the steeds, an impressive creature with a scar beneath one eye. Its nostrils flare with impatience. It tosses its mane restlessly.

These undersea creatures are exaggeratedly stunning. It is well, mid night when we arrive at the great hill at the palace of Elburg.
There are dozens of the folk here, crowding around the entrance to the vast throne room where court is being held.
It was so amazing to see kinds of creatures yet with human appeal, elegant, green-skinned ladies in long gowns, laughing boys, a boy in a shark mask, an elderly woman with jelly fish crowding her shoulders; a gaggle of girls with wild coral reefs in their hair, a bark-skinned boy with fins. Many I've seen before; a few I've spoken with.

I know I shouldn't love it as I do, stolen as I am from the mortal world, parents murdered. But I love it all the same.
Well, High king had a meeting with all the

subordinate kings and knights in his meeting hall. Here the music starts and every creature started to dance. My leather slipper hit the ground like a slap. Tulie comes to us to remind not to dance. But I don't give a chance to her, so I took Maria with me and dissolved in the crowd of palace.

The High king has three heirs. And they three are said to be have their own characteristics. *Baranian* , the first heir of high king is said to be so powerful. Prince *Frain* being the middle son of high king, is said to have a good command over the army and in defence. Prince *Eric* the youngest son of high king, whom I hate the most is in my class still studying undersea school. Eventually the ceremony ends and we are followed to Haleth's court.

As the night breaks, I open the windows to my bedroom and let the last of the cool night air flow in as I strip of my court dress. I feel hot all over. My skin feels too tight, and my heart won't stop racing, on thought, that the next day I have to go to undersea school, the place where

I hate and the place where I am ill treated for being a mortal human.

I find bath water waiting for me, but it has gone tepid. Servants must have come and gone. I climb in any way and splash my face. Living in under sea, it's impossible not to notice that everyone else smells like verbana and sulphury. I smell like pit sweat and sour breath unless I scrub myself clean.

When miss Roa comes into light the lamps, she finds me dressing for a lecture, which begins in the late afternoons and stretches on into some evenings. I wear grey leather boots and a tunic with Haleth's crest...a dagger, crescent moon turned on its side so, it rest like a cup and the single drop of blood falling from one corner embroidered in silk thread.
Downstairs, I find Maria at the banquet table, alone, nursing a cup of nettle tea and picking at a bannock.
Haleth insists-perhaps out of guilt or shame- that we be treated like the children of under- sea. That we take the same lessons that we be given whatever they have. Genny used to go with us, but then she became bored and didn't bother.

Maria and I set off, swinging our baskets. We go past through the far corner of the milkwood, picking our way, passing the pale silvery trunk and bleached shells. From there, we spot mermaids and merrows sunning themselves near cragy caves, their scales reflecting the amber glow of the late afternoon sun.

All the children of undersea, regardless of age, are thought by lecturers from all over the kingdom on the grounds of the palace. Some afternoons we sit in groves carpeted with emerald moss, and other evening we spend in high towers or up in trees. We learn about the medicinal and magical properties of herbs, the language of fishes and aqua flowers and people as well as the language of the folk, the composition of riddles. I like the lessons. Answering the lecturers cleverly in something no one can take from me, even if the lecturers themselves occasionally pretend otherwise.

Haleth trained me to be formidable even with a wooden sword. Maria isn't bad, either, even though she doesn't bother practicing anymore. At the summer tournament, in only a few days, our mock war will take place in front of the royal family. The winner of the tournament or the one who gets the attention of the royal king might be chosen for knighthood. It would be a kind of power, kind of protection. However, Haleth is never going to allow us for such a tournament.

When we reach at school, Prince *Eric, Finch, Lunet* and *Andrea* are already sprawled in the coral grass with few other undersea creatures. We spread our blanket and set out our note books and pens and pot of ink.
Our lesson involves the history of the delicately negotiated peace between Siren, once the queen of the undersea and the various undersea kings and queens of the water.
As the afternoon drowns, Maria and I unpack our baskets from home, which contain bread, butter, cheese and plumps. I butter a piece of bread hungry.
Passing us, Eric kicks dirt onto my food right before I put it into my mouth. The other undersea creatures laugh.
I look up to see him watching me with cruel delight, like a raptor bird trying to decide whether to be bothered devouring small mouse. He's wearing a high collar tunic embroidered with thorns his fingers heavy with rings. His sneer is well practiced.
I grit my teeth.

"Dirt! It's what you came from mortal. It's what you will return to soon enough. Take a big bite "since Eric is a prince, it's more than likely no one has ever cautioned him. Lunet, being the friend of Eric "you do still eat that do you?"asks with mock sympathy as he kicks more dirt on to our lunch.

Andrea pulls a pin from my hair, causing one of my braids to fall against my neck.

"What's this?"She is holding up the glittery pin, with a tiny cluster at the top. "Did you steal it? Did you think it would make your beautiful? Did you think it would make you as we are?"

I bite the inside of my cheek. Of course I want to be like them. They are beautiful. They will live forever. They aren't like us, they don't have death naturally, until someone kills them.

"You'll never be our equal", Andrea says.

Of course I won't, but this arrogance hate this, even though we aren't folk of undersea but at least we are living beings, and here Prince Eric and his friends never ever remember this. They always annoy us. They treat us more insulting than servants.

Although some of the royal kings of undersea had humans as their servants, they bring their maids and workers from our world. But here we aren't any workers. We are likely the step

children of Haleth, one of king from royal
dysentery. But we are powerless here. This is
what hurts me the most. That's why I want to
take part in summer tournament and show them,
I'm too not weak, but much more powerful than
them.
"Oh, come on" Finch says "let them leave to
their misery"
"Sia's sorry," Maria says quickly. "We are both
really sorry".
"She can show us how sorry she is," Eric drawls.
"Tell her she doesn't belong in the summer
tournament"
"Afraid I'll win?" I ask which isn't smart.
"It's not for mortals" he informs us, voice chilly.
I open my mouth, but Maria speaks before I can.
"I'll talk to her about it." She holds my hand and
takes me out of the place.

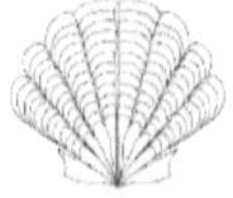

On our way home Maria stops and picks some
mulberries. I sit on a rock deliberately do not
look at anything. "Don't act stupid, you know
what might they can do with us "she scolds me
"Have you forgotten what they have done with

you last time?"
She reminds me of the incident, happened some months ago, when I went home unconsciously breathless, because Eric has mixed up the kelp salt with my food, by which mortals can lose their ability to survive undersea even after taking coral pollen. I was going to die, but Finch, helped me with some of the magical plants. This is why I want power so badly. For that I have to win the summer tournament.
"Are you going to quit the tournament?"Maria asks.
"No I'm going to win it at any cost" i say.
"If you are so sure Haleth is going to give you permission, why haven't you asked him yet?" Maria whispers. "the tournament is only three days away."
Anyone can fight in the summer tournament, but if I want to be a knight, I must declare my candidacy by wearing a green sash across my chest. And if Haleth will not allow me that, then no amount of skill will help me. I haven't asked Haleth because I am afraid of what he will say.
We get home, pushing open the enormous wooden door with its looping iron work. I and Maria, we head straight over rooms. I feel so tired.
At dinner table we sit at a massive table curve along all four sides. Servants bring silver plates

piled with food. Haleth and Tulie drink Canary wine, we children mix it with water. Hue giggles.
"You should know that high king will soon abdicate his throne in favour of one of his children," Haleth says, looking at all of us. "It is likely that he will choose Prince Frain "
"The New kings coronation will be at the autumn solstice." He says.
"What about the next king of your court?"Maria sighs; Haleth looks at Genny, Tulie looks unhappy.
We all knew that Genny is going to be the commander of his court. But what about Hue, Tulie might have obligation with that.
I am wondering what his plan might be, when Maria kicks me under the table. When I turn to glare at she raises both brows. "Ask him" she mouths.
Haleth looks in her direction. "Yes?"
"Sia wants to ask you something, "Maria says. The worst part is, I think she believes she is helping.
I take a deep breath. At least he seems to be in a good mood. "I've been thinking about the tournament." I imagined saying these words many, many times, but now that I am actually doing it, they don't seem to come out the way I planned. "I'm not bad with a sword."

"You do yourself too modest," Haleth says. "Your bladesmanship is excellent."

That seems encouraging. I look over at Maria, who appears to be holding her breath. Everyone at the table has gone still except for Hue, who taps his glass against the side of his plate.
"I am going to fight in the Summer Tournament, and I want declare myself ready to be chosen for knighthood."
Haleth's brows go up. "That's what you want? It's dangerous work."

I nod. "I'm not afraid."

"Interesting," he says. My heart thuds dully in my chest. I have thought through every aspect of this plan except for the possibility that he won't allow it.

"I want to make my own way at the Court," I say.

"You're no killer," he tells me. I flinch, my gaze coming up to his. He looks back at me steadily with his golden cat eyes.
"Fight in the tournament if you like, for sport, but you will not put on the green sash.
I am still confused has he given me permission

for tournament or he cut me off from knighthood.

I want to scream at him: do you know how hard it is to always keep your head down? To swallow insults and endure our right threads? And yet I have done so.

He has no idea what I am.

"Prince frain will make a fine king," Tulie says, deftly shifting the conversation back to pleasant things.

The summer tournament is being held on the edge of a cliff. It's far enough that I take amount appeal grey horse.

A crowd is already gathering around the tinted box where the high king and the rest of the royals will sit. The decadent eldest son, Prince Baranian, is sprawled in a carved chair, three attendants around him.

If I don't try too hard today, at least I never need know if I would have been good enough.

My group is to go first because we are the youngest. Still in training. using wooden swords instead of live steel, unlike those who follow us. As I approach the other students with their practice swords, I her my name whispered. Unnerved, I look around, only to realize I am being scrutinized in a new way. Maria and I are always noticeable, being mortal, but what makes us stand out is also what makes us unworthy of much regard. Today, however, that's not so. The children of undersea seem to be holding a single indrawn breath, waiting to see what my punish-ment will be for putting hands on Eric the day before. Waiting to see what I am going to do next.

I look across the field at Eric and his friends, with silver on their arms. Eric is wearing silver on his chest, too, a plate of gleaming steel that hooks over his shoulders.
I drink some water out of a pewter carafe set out for participants and I begin to warm up. My stomach is saw with the lack of food but I know longer feel hungry. I feel sick, eaten up with nerves.

And then it is time. We troop onto the field and salute the seat of the High King, although high king has not yet arrived. The crowd is thinner than it will be closer to sunset. Prince Frain is there, though, with Madoc beside him. Genny and Maria have come to watch, although I see neither Tulie nor Hue.

Maria watches me intently, as though trying to warn me with her gaze.

All through the first battle, I fight defensively. I avoid Eric. Nor do I come near Andrea, Lunet or Finch.

Still, I do nothing.

Then we are called to the field for the second battle.

Eric walks behind me. "You are docile today. Did your sister admonish you? She desires our approval very much."

My good intentions evaporate on the wind. My blood is on fire, boiling in my veins, I do not have much power, but here is what I have-I can force his hand. Eric might want to hurt me, but I can make him want to hurt me worse. We're supposed to play at war. When they call us to our places, I play. I play as viciously as possible. My practice sword cracks against Eric's ridiculous chest plate. My shoulder bangs against Lunet's shoulder so hard that he staggers back. I attack again and again, knocking down anyone wearing a silver armband. When the mock war is over, my eye is blackened and both of my knees are skinned and the gold side has won the second and third battles.

The crowd applauds, Genny salutes me with a goblet. Haleth is no longer in the royal box. Baranian is gone too. The high king is there though, sitting on a slightly elevated platform, speaking with Frain, his expression remote.

I start to tremble all over, the adrenaline draining out of me. No one seems particularly impressed. I have done my best, have fought my hardest, and it wasn't enough. Haleth didn't even stay to watch.

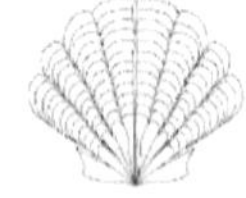

The rest of the summer tournament goes by in a blur.

I ride home alone. Genny heads off to hunting in the nearby Woods. Maria agrees to accompany her, but I am too weary and too Sore and too on edge.

In the kitchens of Haleth's house, I toast cheese over a fire and spread it on bread. Sitting on the stoop with that and a mug of tea. When I am done, I brush crumbs from my

cheeks and head for my room.
Garreth, a servant with long ears and a tail that drags on the ground, stops in the hall when he sees me. He's carrying a tray of thimble-size shell cups and a silvery decanter.
"Oh,you are at home," he says, a growl in his voice that makes him you seem menacing no matter how benign the words he speaks.
I nod.
"The prince is asking for you downstairs."

Eric, here? My heartbeat speeds. I can't think.
"Where?" Garreth looks surprised by my reaction. "In Haleth's study. I was just bringing him this-"
I fly down the stairs and kick open the door to Haleth's's study room.
Prince Frain has several books lying open on the library table in front of him. He raises both eyebrows. "Sia. I didn't expect you to be in such a rush."I sink into a low bow and hope he will think me only clumsy. Fear gnaws at me, sharp and sudden. Could Eric have sent him? Is he here to punish me for insolence? I can think of no other reason that honored and honorable Prince Frain, soon to be the ruler of undersea, would ask for me.
He sits up straighter, as though I am suddenly

much more interesting. "I thought maybe one of my brothers was bothering you." I shake my head. "Nothing, like that."
"It's shocking." he says, as though he's giving me some great compliment. "I know humans can lie, but to watch you do it is incredible. Do it again."
I am breathing too shallowly, too fast.

Frain, about to be crowned the High King, has the power to grant me a place in the Court, the power to gainsay Haleth and make me a knight. If only I could impress him, he could give me everything I want. Everything I thought I lost my shot at.

The prince tilts his head to study me. He asks me as if he had read my mind "You no need to impress me anymore, I'm already influenced with your fight with my brother in mock war."
I blink confused.
"Tell me what you dream of ,Sia, girl of mortal land."
My heart hammers in my chest, and I feel a little light-headed, a little dizzy. Surely it can't be this easy. Prince Frain, soon to be the High King of all undersea, asking me what I want. I barely dare answer, and yet I must.

"I-I want to be your knight," I stammer.
His eyebrows go up. "Unexpected," he says. "And pleasing. What else?"
"I don't understand." I twist my hands.
"But I'm here to make a deal with you" he waves off my answer. I wonder what might be the deal, that prince himself came to ask me.
"Although we are brothers, we are very different from each other. I will never be cruel to you for the sake of delighting in it. If you swear yourself into my service, you will find yourself rewarded. But what I want you for is not knighthood."
My heart sinks. If he doesn't want me to be a knight then what he want me to be? I am still confused and I am still in wonder. What might be I will rewarded of? "Then what do you want?" I asked in a polite yet startled way.

"Nothing you haven't already offered. You wanted to give me your oath and your sword. I accept. I need someone who can lie, someone with ambition. Spy for me. Join my *Mob of dark web*.I can make you powerful beyond what you might ever hope. It's not easy for humans to be here with us. But I could make it easier for you."
A spy. A sneak. A liar and a thief. Of course that's what he thinks of me, of mortals. Of

course that's what he thinks I am good for.
"I don't think it might lower you. But i have seen your talent and your war skills, you must not be directly represented as a knight. You could do much more than that."
"What is the Mob of dark web mean?" I go still.

" You too know, I'm going be thrones as high king. Recently I've know from Haleth that i have a life threat. Perhaps you already know, how close and dearest is Haleth for me so he cautioned me. I was really searching for someone, so I created a secret group of spies, who can spy for me but no undersea creature had the skills you have. I'm really impressed."
He may be complimenting me.
"So you accept?" He nods once.
It's frightening to have a choice like this in front of me, a choice that changes all future choices.
I want power so badly. And this is an opportunity for it, a terrifying and slightly insulting opportunity. But, also an intriguing one.
I nod and hope I make a good spy.
"Sia, the creature of land, from this day forward no undersea glamour will addle your mind."
"Now no one will be able to control you," he says

and then pauses for a moment "except me."
I suck in a breath.
And yet, it is still thrilling to have any protection
at all. Prince Frain is only one undersea king, and
he has seen something in me, something Haleth
wouldn't see, something I have yearned to have
acknowledged.

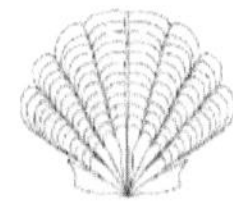

I go to sleep early, and when I wake, it is full
dark. My head hurts- I maybe from sleeping too
long-and my body aches. I must have slept with
all my muscles tensed.
The lectures of that day have already begun. It
doesn't matter. I'm not going.

Roa has left me a tray with coffee on it, spiced
with cinnamon and cloves and a little bit of
pepper. I pour a cup. It's lukewarm, which means
it has been there for a while. There's toast, too,
which softens up when I dunk it a few times.
Then I wash my face, I brush my hair roughly,
and then I pull it into a bun by knotting it around

a twig.

I refuse to think about what happened the day before. I refuse to think about anything but today and my mission for Prince Frain.

I go to prince Frain's Hollow hall, without getting caught by anybody. I myself feel that I'm capable of it, by passing all the tight security of upcoming high king without getting caught. I think this is why he chosen me as a spy. When he saw me, no wonder on his face. But he says, "oh, you've come. I know you'll cross all things despite of the problem. I guess no one has seen you coming here"

"Yeah none noted me" I nod.

He's about to say something, suddenly a creature enters Frain's room. I ought to hide but he says me to b relaxed. A male creature, his skin the green of ponds. His nose is long and twists fully around, before bending back toward his face like a scythe.

"They call me *Club*," he says, his voice melodious, completely at odds with his face. He bows and then cocks the side of his head toward Frain.

"At his service. I guess we both are. You're the new girl, right?"

I nod.

Prince Frain introduces me to *Club*, "He'll take you to the Mob of dark web and tell you what to do."

I follow the Club, through the palace, keeping back from him a few steps so it doesn't seem like we're together. We pass a general Haleth knows, and I make sure to keep my head bowed. I don't think he would look closely enough to recognize me, but I cannot be sure.

"Where are we going?" I whisper after several minutes of walking through the halls.

"Just a little farther," he says gruffly, opening a cupboard and climbing inside. "Well, come on close the door." He grunts.

The Roach opens the door, and light floods the hallway, causing me to throw my arm up in front of my face. Blinking, I look into the secret lair of Prince Frain's spies.

A large table dominates the room, and sitting at it are two undersea creatures I've never met both of them gazing at me unhappily.

"Welcome," says the Club, "to the Mob of dark web."

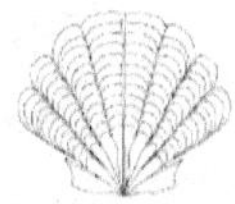

The two other members of Frain's spy troupe also have code names.

There is the lean, handsome creature that looks at least part human, who winks and tells me to call him the *spirit*.

The other is a tiny delicate girl her skin the dapple the brown of a doe and a cloud of white around her head. "I'm the *Cyanide*" she says.

I am at a loss as to how to speak with them. "so is it just the three of you?"

"Four now" says the club.

"Well we all know why we are here, to gather information and to overthrow the coming threat on our prince, so we must...." Club continues his speech, but i don't know what to do.

"Who must have been trying to kill Frain?" I question stupidly.

"Its well known that upcoming king though have alot of enemies " says club.

" But why would high king have decided to throne Frain while, prince Baranian is the eldest heir of his gentry?" I know i spoke smart.

"Oh, yes it a mark of question, but Baranian is abolished from coronation. Because he is accused to be the killer of high king's consort. That's why he is resisted from being crowned." Club tells me.

"Now it's your turn Sia, to show us how capable you are to spy. You must start your work right now. You go to high king's court and there do your work in Baranian's room" he addresses me what to do and tells me the way to Baranian's room in high king's court is in the last corner. I go to the high king's court, obviously I'm a spy, I pass through, the servants the guards.

However in the disguise of a servant i enter upstairs and look up for the corner room, i see the walls are stone and hung with no paintings or tapestries. A massive half-tester bed takes up most of the space in the first room.
Along the wall are more books, some of them familiar from Haleth's library.

The seventh room enters into a hallway with stairs spiraling up and up into what must be the tower. I take them quickly, my heart racing, my leather shoes soft on the stone. I think this must be the Baranian's room. As I guess this is in the corner.

There's a huge table dominating the middle of the room, and on it are maps weighed down on the corners by chunks of glass and metal objects. Beneath them is correspondence.
 I shuffle through the papers until I come to this letter:

I know the provenance of the cuttle sea apple,
that   you asked for, but whatever you do with it must
not be tied with me.

Although the letter seems old and unsigned, I
remember Tulie always warning Hue not to eat
Sea apples without knowing their species.
 I think this cuttle specie might be a poison. I
think Prince Baranian wants to kill Frain through
poisoning his food. I must warn Frain. I don't
know I'm thinking is right or not but I can't
take a chance. The mob of dark web always
suspected Baranian. I guess what I found is
really important.
I wanted to take the letter with me, but I don't
want Baranian to find his letter lost, I start to
copy that.
I'm almost done I hear a sound. People are
coming upstairs. I panic. No place for me to hide.
There's practically nothing to hide. I jump off
the window.
My eyes open into the slits of grass. Even though
I feel my body aching but I feel safe.
I must go to the mob and inform them, but it's
too late I have to go to home.

I fall asleep in the bath area of my room, spread out on the floor. That's where the Spirit finds me."Rise Sia" the Spirit says. He has come to know about me. I push myself up, too exhausted to disobey.
I tell him everything I have seen and spy yesterday from Baranian's room. He doesn't get shocked and insist me that their guess on Baranian's intentions to kill Frain is clear. He says "you rest up for the day, i go and Inform our mob about this then you later go to Frain and alert him." I obey his instructions.

I wake up groggy. Prince Frain awaits downstairs in General Haleth's parlor. I wonder has he come for me or for Haleth?. If it's for me, we can't meet publicly. I run down stairs, he's having a discussion with Haleth. I was correct he is here to talk with Haleth.
I go up my room and make myself. I plan to meet him this evening and tell him about the cuttle sea apple.
The evening had came up. I see Spirit coming in

my room through window. The spirit gives me a vague look. He seemed to be tensed up. I ask what happened."I can't find Club and Cyanide. I searched them everywhere, but my work gone in vain. Have you informed it to Frain?" he asked. " No this morning I saw Frain going out with Haleth and wanted to meet him this evening. I'm just getting upto go to him, come with me"

He follows me. We have reached the court of Prince Frain. But he isn't there. Where might he have gone? I think I can't meet him today too. I went back home, leaving spirit in mob room. Table was ready with food. Maria asked me where i was all the day and i have not even went to school. Genny giggled, "she seems to have made new friends and she is busy with them". I give a vague smile.
Tulie's busy with Hue. I can't see Haleth on the table. I guess he is not in home too. I ask "where is Haleth?" Tulie unwantedly answers me,
"Tonight he's having dinner with prince Frain and Baranian"
My Brain blocked. What might be a dinner with Baranian be? That too when Haleth is close friend of Frain. I guess Baranian not only wants to kill Frain but also Haleth. I must stop them.
" I must go " I shout and I run away without

even thinking what might Tulie, Maria and Genny thinks.
I run to to Mob room to find my co-spy s. But I found none there. May be Spirit too have taken leave. I don't know what to do,where to go and whom to tell.
I run to High king's court. I make myself look like a undersea creature. I'm really in a hurry and i lost my consciousness I was not able to hide myself form the guards, I wanted to meet high king, i run from the guards and pull up the Alert knob. Which rings all over the Elburg, all the folk of undersea, every general, every king, each and every person of royal family alerts at the high king's court. When I look out of high king's palace I see a large crowd gathered there for the call of high king. I can see Frain and Haleth too there in his court. I guess I was on time. Otherwise I wouldn't have seen them alive with Baranian. I manage to cope up with High king. I tell him everything, all about the plan of Baranian.

High king was not such rude as i thought. But he is so logical. He announced everyone that, the prince Frain's coronation will be preponed and it will be held in just two days. It mean the day after the next day.

I'm shocked. Have my actions make sense? what have I done. was i correct? or over dramatic to pull up the Alert knob.
But no one knows it was me, the reason for the preponing of Frain's crowning.

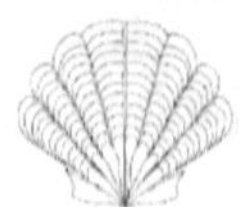

The dressmaker comes early the next afternoon, a long-fingered creature called *Bamberfelt*. Her feet are turned backward, her odd gait. She is wearing an example of her work, a woven dress with embroidered lines of thorns making a striped pattern down the length of it. She has brought with her bolts of dresses of different fabrics. All dresses are draped onto the couch in Tulie's parlor for us to inspect. Even Genny is drawn to run her fingers over the cloth, an absent smile on her face. There is nothing like this in the mortal world, and she knows it.

I pour myself tea and drink it without cream, hoping it will settle my stomach.
The memory of the cuttle sea apple keeps rising unbidden to my mind, what might have happened

if I haven't ringed the alert knob. I'm lost in my thoughts.

"Sia?" Tulie says, and I realize that I've been staring off toward the window and the fading light.

"Yes?" I put on a bright, false smile. Maria and Genny begin to laugh.

"And just who are you thinking about with a dreamy expression like that on your face?" Tulie asks, which makes Genny laugh again. Maria doesn't, probably because she thinks I am an idiot.

I shake my head, hoping I have not gone red-faced. "No, it wasn't anything like that. I was just-I don't know. It doesn't matter. What were we talking about?"

I look over Bamberfelt who holds gowns to show us up.

I am going to get a pretty gown. I will dance at Prince Frain's coronation until my feet bleed.

After all I am going to get enormous power.

I focus my attention on the cloth until I can breathe evenly again, until the panic dissipates. There's a velvet blue-green, reminding me of the lake at dusk. I find an amazing, fantastical fabric embroidered with sea stars and shells and ferns and flowers. I lift it up, and underneath is

a bolt of beautiful fog-gray cloth that ripples like smoke. They're so very pretty. The kind of fabrics that princesses in fairy tales wear. Maria choses different cloth, the dark blue velvet gown. Genny choses a violet that seems to be a silvery grey when she turns into over her hand. Tulie choses a bluish pink gown for herself and cricket green coloured dress for Hue.
Haleth called me and Maria in his study room.

"Has your dress selection completed?" He asks us.
"Yes" nods Maria. I follow up her looks.
"I wanted to give you this, "he took out a sword, my heart melted on seeing that It's really, really, really a pretty sword.
"It's maker called it *Shadowshard*" he said.
"I'm confused whom to give it in both of you" he utters.
"But why do you want to give us?" I ask.
"That's good, because this is your sword by right, forged for me by your father, *Justin*. He's the one who crafted it, the one who named it. It's your family heirloom."

I am momentarily robbed of breath. I have never heard my father's name spoken aloud by Haleth before. We do not talk about the fact

that he commanded his sister to murder my parents; we talk around it.
We certainly don't talk about when they were alive. "My father made this," I say carefully, to be sure. "My father was here, in undersea?"
"Yes, for several years. I only have a few pieces of his. I found only one for you" He grimaces.

"This is where your mother met him. Then they ran away together, back to the mortal world."
"She was clever, your mother. And young. After I brought her to undersea, she drank and danced weeks away at a time. She was at the center of every revel.
I could not always accompany her. There was a war in the East, an Unseelie king with a lot of territory and no desire to bend his knee to high king. I had to go, but at that time she was carrying Genny in her womb. I don't wanted to leave her like that so accompanied my sister Dolreth, from sea land to look after her. She was her responsibility.
Your father was interesting. He was a master smith when he came here and even better when he left. But he couldn't resist bragging about stealing our secrets along with his bride.
After the war I found my wife to be lost, my unborn child to be taken away, my sister to be

unconscious.
At that time my sister Dolreth vowed me that she will bring back my heir to me at any way."
He tells the untold story, happened before the beginning.
Maria, i don't know what's going in her mind, tells,"i think Sia must own this sword" and she leaves."Yes," I say, unable to help myself. When I pull it from its sheath, it comes as though made for my hand.
He leaves I hold head. My thoughts will not focus. When I me. my rise, though, I strap on my new sword. It is cold and solid in heavy as a promise.
Although the next day is going to be a very big day.

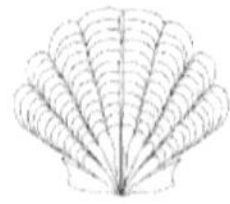

Finally the day of crowning has come.

Bells begin to ring, signaling the start of the ceremony. The musicians quiet their fiddles and harps. For a long moment, the hill is silent, listening, and then people move to their places. I push toward the front, where the rest of the Gentry of the High King's Court are assembling. Where, my family will be. Tulie is there already, standing beside one of Haleth's best knights and looking as though she wishes she could be anywhere else. Hue is off his leash and on Maria's shoulders. Genevieva has come out of the crowd, cat eyes agleam, hair loose around her face.

Instead, I hang back, watching the royal family assemble on the dais. The High King is seated on his throne of woven branches, wearing the heavy circlet, looking out from his deeply lined face with alert bronze eyes, like those of an owl. Prince Frain sits on a humble wooden stool beside him, dressed in all-white robes, his feet and hands bare. And behind the throne stands the rest of the royal family-Baranian. Even *Toinot*, Prince Frain's mother, is present, in a garment of shining gold. The only family member missing is Eric.

The High King stands and the entire place goes quiet. "Long has been my rule, but today I take my leave of you." His voice echoes through the land and water. The assembled Folk speak as one, surprising me. "We release you," they say, words echoing around me.

The High King lets his heavy robe of state fall from his shoulders. It crumples on the stone in a jewel-encrusted pile. He takes the shell crown from his own head. Already, he stands up straighter. There is an unnerving eagerness in him. He has been the High King of Elburg longer than the memories of many of the Folk.

"Whom will you put in your stead, to be our High King?" Martyr asks. "My second-born, my son Frain," says High king. "Come forward, child." Prince Frain rises from his humble place on the stool. His mother removes the white cloth covering him, leaving him naked.

The High King speaks. "Come, Frain. Kneel before me."

The Crown Prince bends down in front of his father and the assemblage.

Martyr voice speaks, "And will Folk of undersea accept Prince Frain as your High King?" The cry rose up from the crowd, in chirping voice "We will."

"I will not accept you," Baranian says. "I have come to challenge you for the crown." All around the dais, I see knights unsheathing blades.

"I need not fight you," Frain says, gesturing out toward the knights grouped thickly around the dais, waiting for an order. Haleth is among them.

"Then have this on your conscience". Baranian walks two steps: and thrusts out his arm. He doesn't even look in the direction he's thrust- ing, but his blade pierces high kings throat. Someone shrieks, then every- one does. For a moment, the wound is just a blotch against her skin, and then blood pours out, a river of red. He staggers forward, going to her hands and knees. Gold fabric and glittering gems are drowning in scarlet.

"Guards," Frain in a voice that expects to be obeyed. None of says, the knights advance toward the dais, though.

The crowd surges, carrying me with it. Everyone is moving, pushing forward or away from the gruesome tableau.

Haleth gets there.
For a brief moment, I am relieved. His commanders' loyalty might be bought, but,

Then Haleth thrusts his sword through Frain's chest with such force that the blade emerges on the other side. He drags it up, through his rib cage, to his heart.
I stop moving and let the crowd flow around me. I am still as stone. I see a flash of white bone, of wet red muscle. Prince Frain, who was almost the High King, falls on top of the gem-crusted red cloak of state, his spilling blood lost in the jumble of jewels.
But I cannot believe that this is Haleth's plan. Frain is his friend. Frain campaigned with him. Frain is going to reward him once he's the High King. But Haleth has coped with Baranian. Baranian has betrayed high king , and Frain is gone, taking all my hopes and plans with him. Haleth's hands are gloved in red. I can't stop staring them.
Baranian orders a knight to bring him crown. Martyr says, "Baranian firstborn, no matter

whose blood you spill, you will never rule Elburg."
"You are unworthy of the crown."
"You killed your family; now you have none to
crown you. You can become king only if the royal
family member crowns you" cautions the Martyr.
"But Toinot, my mother is alive she will crown
me" Baranian's arrogance speaks.
Toinot helplessly had to crown but.... Taniot's
horned head rolls a short ways until it hits
Frain's corpse.
The spirit killed her, spy from mob of dark web,
he killed her. He never wanted Baranian to be
king. But he should not have done this.
"No!" I shout, although my voice is drowned out
by the crowd.
"You have three days to get it onto your head, or
else three days later the crown's power will
depart" Martyr says.
" I have my brother Eric, he will crown me, he
has the power to crown me" Baranian orders
Haleth to find Eric.
But Eric is not found anywhere.

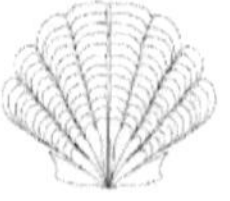

There is blood on my dress, little dots of it
sinking into the blue sky. I thought I could not
be shocked by death, but-there was just so
much of it. An embarrassing, ridiculous excess.
My mind keeps going back over Prince Frain's
white ribs.
I think of Haleth, who had been at Frain's right
hand all these years. Undersea creatures might
not be able to lie outright, but Haleth had lied
with every laugh, every clap on the back, every
shared cup of wine.
At least knights had led my family away before
the killing started. At least none of the others
had to watch, although, unless they were very
far away, they could not have failed to hear the
screams.

Eric. The only one who can legitimately crown

Baranian. The only other descendant of the royal king left. Everyone in Elburg must be looking for him.

And here he is, wandering around in a flimsy silver fox half mask, blinking at me with drunken confusion and swaying a bit on his feet. I almost laugh outright. Imagine my luck to be the one to find him.

I press the tip of Shadowshard, the sword of my father, against his skin so he can feel the bite. The most important boy in undersea and my enemy, finally in my power. It feels even better than I thought it would. His black eyes focus on me with new intensity. "Why?" he asks. "Because your luck is terrible and mine is great. Do what I say, you are under my control now." The power to crown the king is under my abduction. I feel great.

I press the knife harder. I shout out *the power is abducted*

"No matter how unlikely it seems you are the most important person in all of undersea. Whosoever has you, has power." I tells him.

The first thing I do is i take him to the mob of

dark web and hide him there. No one else is there. It doesn't matter. I can manage without them.

I return to home. It's a long walk through the woods, longer because I give the encampments of the Folk here for the coronation a wide berth. My dress is dirty and tattered at the hem, my feet are sore and cold.

In the hall, I see that there are more knights here than I am used to, coming in and out of Haleth's parlor. Servants rush back and forth, bringing tankards and inkpots and maps. Few spare me a look.

Hue is in bed, Tulie and Maria are outside Haleth's study room and Genny is up in the balcony.

I'm still confused just a night before i was told about my parent's truth then i ignored everything just because I was going to get power after prince Frain's coronation. But how can everything change in one night.

I want to scream. I want to run at him, I feel like a child again, a helpless child in a house of death.

I want to do something, but I do nothing.

I go back to mob of dark web. There I found my co-spy s. The Club, Cyanide and Spirit. It somewhat felt like a moment of relaxation. Well, they knew everything happened and i gues they might know what to do next.

The club appreciates me for abducting Prince Eric. The group of spy is happy that Baranian has not become king but we lost Frain. it's so ridiculous.

The spirit tells me," I think our next step is so efficient we can't decide anything without any reason. It would be better if we find any information about Baranian." Cyanide reflectingly,"yes, Sia could do that she again have to enter Baranian's room once I"

I'm exhausted, "how can I spy a betrayal who is in search of his own brother, how can I enter his room?" I tell.

The spirit smartly suggest, "that's what the point is, he is busy in searching his brother everywhere, what if you hide him in his own room. Common Sia you can do this, we cant take risk just two days left for the crown to lose its power. So Baranian will try his best to find Eric. But you have to do this. Only you can do this."

I take a deep breath and decide that if I am really going to do this, I could use some help.

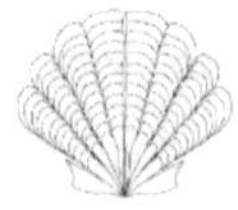

Twenty minutes later, I light the stub of a candle and make my way to the room where Eric has been tied up. I see him, he's still unconscious. It has been eight hours that i have given him poke weed , undersea creatures should not take poke weed it make them unconscious for more than ten hours. I just have two hours of time to make the way to Baranian's room until he wakes up.

The monarchs of other Courts, along with the wild unallied undersea creatures who came for the coronation, had made camp on the

easternmost corner of the high king's court.
They had pitched tents, some in motley, some in
diaphanous silks. When get close, I can see fires
burning. Honey wine and spoiled meat perfume
the air.
I have made Eric look like a mortal girl
servant,he seems so funny I can't stop my laugh
that I've made a prince as a girl servant. I too
dressed in a servant's gown.

This time I enter high king's home from the
back side, the place where I have jumped off
from Baranian's room. It's the exact place to
directly enter in his room. I make clear that no
one is around there, some of the guard are at
Haleth's home, some with Baranian some at
school and some searching Eric through all the
undersea.
However, i enter the room from the window but
it was so hard to carry a unconscious mortal girl
dressed prince. His face still makes me laugh.
Although, I'm in his room now. No one is at high
king's home. It's so empty.

I don't know when I have slept, until Eric wakes me up with his sounds as he is tied up. I'm so drowsy, but he is in full conscious. He has neither drunk now nor he had the effect of pokeweed. He grins at me. He start to shout out loud. I don't know what to do. Although I'm in Baranian's room, I can't take risk what if any of the maids sees me here with him. In confusion i punch on his face. It was so hard punch but it was just to calm him down yet I hated him from my school.

I don't understand what ima doing, i panic and talk to him softly," I'll tell you everything you just calm down."

He roughly stares at me. His gaze meets mine. I wonder how would he calm down just on my words. But whatever his calmness favors me and I'm ok with that.

"But why are we here, at Frain's room? How have I come here?" He asks me.

I start to tell him everything. But wait Frain's room?

"What you mean Frain's room?"I ask.

"Yes, it's my brother Frain's room. Why are we here and how have you came here?" He continues.

"How could it be Frain's room? It's Baranian's" I tell him which is effortlessly incorrect.

"Baranian's room is in the corner not this" he says.

"But corner room is this itself" i tell him.

"No it isn't the corner. "He utters.

Wait. I go out and find a room in corner.

That mean i was wrong, the room i entered was Frain's then the letter of cuttle sea apple i found must be Frain's. That means Frain wanted to kill???

But whom he wanted to kill???? My stream of questions breaks through the boundaries.

"Would you tell me what has happened??" Eric shouts.

I'm still in shock; I subconsciously tell him everything that happened; About the death of his Father high king, his mother, his brother.

He doesn't even get wondered. He took it so easy. How can someone feel nothing even after knowing his parents death and his own brother's betrayal.

"Don't you feel anything?" I ask him.

" This was expected to happen, but it happened too early only because my father has preponed the ceremony" he says.

"How could you expect your own family's death? How could you be so cruel? Have you known this all earlier?" I question him.

"Obviously, the 1st heir Baranian must be the king, but my father wanted to make Frain king so this must be expected "

"You too know that Baranian is accused of high king's consort, then why would he become king?" I desperately ask.

" Oh..this is what everyone knows but the fact is Frain has killed her and he manipulated high king that Baranian had did that." He says which should not be true.

"But why would Frain kill her?"i want to know the truth.

"I too don't know, you can find it's answer only at your home "

"What?? At my home?? what do you mean?"

"The high king's consort was Tulie's sister " he

says

What, what, what i can't handle this, everything is running out of my mind.

"I too wanted to know, come lets go and ask Tulie" he wants to join me.

"But you can't come with me. If anyone sees you...."

But I think I have to go and know the truth. I must go at night. I can't take risk. I can't take him with me. But I can leave him here unconscious, and hide him.

I give him food mixed with pokeweed. Poor prince Eric, hungrily eats it and takes a long nap. I wait for night. After this night there will just be a single day and until then if I can stop Eric to reach Baranian, the crown will lose its power. I have to do it.

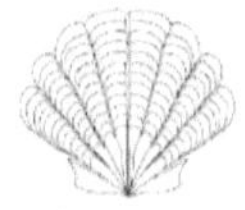

I have to go to home. It's been two days i haven't gone. All are busy in search of Eric that no one cared about me. I reach home. Not well dressed, my hair too isn't braided. "What have you made yourself looked like?" Genny shouts at me. "Where have you been last two days?" Maria hugged me.

I ask "where is Tulie?"

"She might be with Hue "they say.

"I have to talk to her" i say. "About what??" Genny screams.

"It's not important, i just wanted to talk her about Hue" I lie to them

"Ok then, she is upstairs." They instruct me.

I run upstairs. I found her in the fourth room. She has been making Hue sleep. I enter her room.

"Where have you been,Sia?" She asks on looking me. I close the door of room. "What are you doing?" She exclaims. " I have no time, it would be better if you tell me, who killed your sister?" I ask arrogantly.

"About which sister?" She acts.

"The consort of high king" I tell her.

"But who have told you?" she asks.

"Prince Eric"

"Is he with you", she wonders. "Don't you know whole undersea is searching for him, where have you hidden him?"
"I'll tell you but answer me first " I can't wait.
" Ok calm down. Yes, high king's consort is my sister but as everyone knows Baranian hasn't killed her, Frain did."
"But why do Frain will?"i desperately ask.
"She was pregnant with Frain's kid. If anyone would have known it then Frain must have been thrown out the kingdom. So he killed my pregnant sister. she was poisoned with cuttle sea apple. And it affected his kid too. So i never allow Hue to eat Cuttle sea apples "she tells.
"That mean, is Hue your sister and Frain's kid?"
"Yes, no one knows it except me and Haleth. Haleth knows the reality of Frain so he supported Baranian.
On that day when I told you that Haleth's going to have dinner with Frain and Baranian, Haleth went there to settle down the matter without any bloodshed but, High king's unexpected decision of preponing the crowning ceremony made them do this.

Now please tell me where is Eric,let everyone calm." She requests me.
"Sure, I will go and get him" I walk my way.

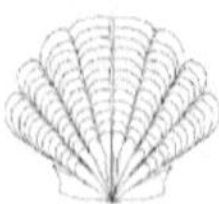

I don't know how to explain what I feel, i have no words. I feel like literally nothing. Nothing's going in my mind. It stopped working.
Just because of my misunderstanding, this all have happened. What if I haven't gone to high king, what if I haven't pulled the alert knob. High king haven't preponed the ceremony, may be Haleth have settled down all the issue between Frain and Baranian, whole royal family would be alive. Everything would have been normal. But it isn't now. I dont understand the mess I've created.
Whatever let me handover Eric to Baranian.
I go back to the place where I have hidden Eric. I didn't find him there. He isn't there. He must have run away I think. But it has happened just 3

hours that i gave him the pokeweed. Still 7 hours for him to wake up. Then where is he? Has the spirit taken him to kill that to never let Baranian become king? No this can't happen now.
I run to the mob of dark web.

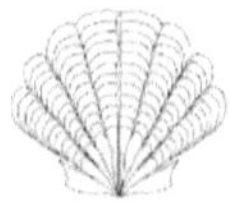

Laughter greets me when I return to the Mob of dark web. I am expecting to find Eric as I left him, unconscious, and perhaps even more miserable than before. Instead, his hands have been untied. Empty and he is at the table, playing cards with the Club, the cyanide.
"How has he come conscious?" I wonder.
"Just with a glass of seaweed wine" Cyanide laughs, club giggles.
"Where's spirit?" I ask
"He has gone to know the current situation of Baranian " Club tells me.
I take deep breath.
"I want to tell you something when spirit arrives,

something important about Frain" I want to tell them the reality of Frain.

" Ok let spirit come" they say while being busy with cards.

I wait and wait. "There's just five more hours to dawn and Baranian will lose the power "Cyanide reminds.

"How could I forget. I came here to handover Eric to Baranian" i shout.

"But why?"they wonder.

"I'll explain it later, i don't have time now" i hurry. I pull Eric to stand but he doesn't obeys me.

All this mess apart.

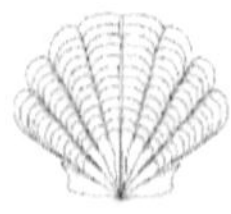

The undersea is vibrating, the scary sounds, strange air, and horror of the shades everywhere. It's like the beginning of the end. The spirit came to us. He's in so hurry. "Run, run, run everyone run" he shouts.

"What has happened?" I scream which is in

audible in such sounds.

"He has arrived "spirit tells. I think he's talking about Baranian. It must be him; Tulie might have told him that i have abducted Eric. So he might be coming here with all of his soldiers i think.

"Let Baranian come, we'll handover Eric to him" i say.

"No it isn't Baranian,"

"Then whom?" I stay still

I see a big monster, ruining the hollow hall. He is so giant, that creature has a long tail with slits, his muscles are well made, his face so disgusting with a middle horn on head. He overall looks like a giant snake. I stand there as a stone.

"Abyss face"they all shout.

Club takes me and run with Cyanide and spirit. I run along them. Eric is left behind.

"Who's this Abyss face?" I ask even though I'm running.

"Abyss face, the rotten serpent. He is a deep sea monster. He is cursed from undersea and he's never allowed here. When Baranian haven't found Eric and the time to dawn is just an hour so he called this monster from the sea. I think he want to ruin everything,he said if he can't have power, no one should have it." Spirit informs me.

My legs running and my mind too. My run stops but not my thinking.

"Just because of me, this monster have arrived. I have to stop him" i say

"He is uncontrollable, don't act foolish Sia just run and save your life" they say.

All my journey from my mortal home to Haleth's home and there to high king's stirs in my mind. It all started for power, if I'm capable of having power i must defeat him. And i will.

I stopped running, the monster stood in front of me, from behind him, Haleth, Tulie, Maria, Genny, everyone shouting me to run. But i can't now. I'm tired of running and saving my life but for what Just to live a powerless life. Now i won't let it happen.

The monster attacks on me with its flippy tail with horns around, but I'm not just a spy but a well trained worrier too. The fight goes on between him and me. It's a restless one.

Although Haleth and Eric comes in my rescue, I wonder why would Eric trying to help me, but this creature is really uncontrollable. Whole the undersea world goes blank when I take out my Shadowshard and thrusts it on the middle horn of his head. There he goes slug. Haleth pierces his sword on its tail, and Eric twists his Rapier in its chest I guess the monster is dead. It falls down the ground making a earthquakic move. Baranian tries to wake him up. He is desperately trying his best to wake it up but after all, the creature has tasted my shot how it could be alive.

When I think of it, Baranian was not such cruel but my actions of misunderstanding lead him to become cruel..may be i was the reason for such betrayal i think but it might be just my opinion. Words in my mind don't have any end.

But, I see Eric nowhere here, where he might be gone.

Everyone in wonder, I see Eric coming with the crown in the hand, now I think after crowning Baranian, everything might become well but......

He's coming towards me, "**People of Undersea, from today onwards the high king of Eiburg is Sia, the warrior of power,**" he crowned me at the last minutes of dawn.

.

I wonder, but yet I could explain the reaction of Elburg people and my family another day.

9 798889 095286